PRIZE PUZZLER

The Hardys and Chet tried some more. Joe stuck his foot onto the cheese for support. No matter how hard they pulled, they couldn't get the sword out of the cheese!

After another minute the boys gave up.

"I thought I was lucky!" Chet groaned.

"Cheer up, Chet," Joe said. "You can't be the big cheese every time."

"Cute," Chet laughed. "Okay, where's my prize ring?"

Joe turned to point at the tree.

"It's right over th—" Joe stopped midsentence. His jaw dropped. The grand prize gold ring that he'd hung on the tree was *gone*!

CATCH UP ON ALL THE HARDY BOYS® SECRET FILES

THE HARDY BOYS®

SECRET FILES #18

Medieval Upheaval

BY FRANKLIN W. DIXON

ILLUSTRATED BY SCOTT BURROUGHS

ALADDIN ▪ NEW YORK LONDON TORONTO SYDNEY NEW DELHI

ALADDIN

An imprint of Simon & Schuster Children's Publishing Division

1230 Avenue of the Americas, New York, NY 10020

First Aladdin paperback edition August 2015

Text copyright © 2015 by Simon & Schuster, Inc.

Illustrations copyright © 2015 by Scott Burroughs

All rights reserved, including the right of reproduction in whole or in part in any form.

ALADDIN is a trademark of Simon & Schuster, Inc., and related logo is a registered trademark of Simon & Schuster, Inc.

THE HARDY BOYS is a registered trademark of Simon & Schuster, Inc.

For information about special discounts for bulk purchases, please contact Simon & Schuster Special Sales at 1-866-506-1949 or business@simonandschuster.com.

The Simon & Schuster Speakers Bureau can bring authors to your live event. For more information or to book an event contact the Simon & Schuster Speakers Bureau at 1-866-248-3049 or visit our website at www.simonspeakers.com.

Series design by Lisa Vega

Cover design by Karina Granda

The text of this book was set in Garamond.

Manufactured in the United States of America 0715 OFF

10 9 8 7 6 5 4 3 2 1

Library of Congress Control Number 2015936397

ISBN 978-1-4814-2269-7 (pbk)

ISBN 978-1-4814-2270-3 (eBook)

CONTENTS

1

Jesters and Jousters

Hey, Frank," eight-year-old Joe Hardy called to his brother. "I just saw two knights in armor, a minstrel, a queen, and a court jester, all in the last five minutes!"

"So?" Frank asked.

"So are you sure we didn't go back in time?" Joe asked with smile.

Nine-year-old Frank pointed to a row of snack stands. "They didn't have slushie machines and

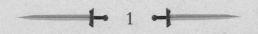

cotton candy in the Middle Ages, did they?" he asked.

"I guess not!" Joe said.

Joe really did know where they were. He and Frank were at the King Arthur Fair. The medieval fair came to Bayport every summer. That was when the park was made to look like a huge marketplace from the days of King Arthur.

There were jugglers, puppeteers, and musicians, all dressed in medieval clothes. But there was only one special Kids Day—and that was today!

"It's cool that Aunt Gertrude left us on our own," Frank said.

Joe nodded. Aunt Gertrude was their dad's sister who lived in the Hardys' garage apartment. Their aunt was fun to be around, but it was also fun to be on their own!

"Now we can do whatever we want here at the

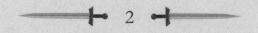

fair," Joe said. "Like enter the Junior Joust. And run through the Medieval Maze!"

"The Medieval Maze?" Frank said with a snort. "Your squirty legs will never get you over the muck pit at the end. You'll be totally covered with mud!"

"Maybe that's what this fair needs," Joe said with a shrug. "A medieval mud monster!"

As the brothers walked on, they passed two knights in armor. One knight's steely glove clanged as he waved.

"We should have dressed up like knights, Frank," Joe said. "Not in these dresses and tights!"

"They're called 'tunics,'" Frank said. "And even knights wore them under their armor."

The brothers were about to check out an acrobat show when they heard the sound of laughter in the distance.

"What's going on?" Joe wondered.

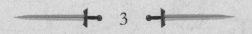

"There's only one way to find out," Frank said. "Let's go!"

Frank and Joe followed the sound to a stage set up between two trees. A banner hanging over the stage read JESTER JOKE SLAM.

"That must be the joke contest!" Joe said. "The winner gets to be Junior Jester of the fair!"

A boy stood onstage, already dressed like a jester. The bells on his cap and shoes jingled each time he moved.

"Hey, I know him!" Frank said. "That's Dougie Skulnick from my class."

A crowd of kids stood before the stage as Dougie shouted out a joke: "Why did King Arthur have a round table?"

"So he wouldn't get cornered!" a boy's voice yelled out.

Frank and Joe would have known that voice anywhere. It belonged to their friend Chet Morton.

They turned to see Chet standing in the crowd next to his sister Iola.

"Uh-oh," Frank whispered. "Chet just gave away Dougie's joke."

"Not cool," Joe sighed.

"Okay," Dougie started again. "Why do dragons sleep during the day?"

"So they can fight knights!" Chet shouted out. "Knights . . . nights . . . Yeah, we get it, Skulnick!"

"We'd better stop Chet," Frank told Joe.

"Yeah," Joe said. "Before he lands up in King Arthur's dungeon!"

Frank and Joe squeezed through the crowd of kids to Chet and Iola. Chet didn't notice the Hardys at first. He was too busy eating a Popsicle and listening to Dougie's next joke:

"What did King Arthur's knights use to get undressed?" Dougie shouted out. "They used—"

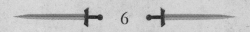

"Can openers!" Chet yelled out. "That joke was on the back of my cereal box!"

The crowd cracked up laughing. But Chet's sister Iola looked mad.

"Zip it, Chet," Iola complained. "Yelling out the answers to jokes isn't cool."

Chet pointed with his Popsicle stick to a gold crown on Iola's head.

"Just because you're wearing a crown doesn't make you queen," Chet told his sister. "Besides, riddles are like mysteries—they're meant to be solved." He finished up his icy treat and noticed his friends.

Chet smiled and waved at Frank and Joe. As detectives, the brothers knew a thing or two about mysteries. They had their own detective headquarters in their tree house, with a Secret Files board to write down all their suspects and clues.

"You'll be sorry, Morton!" Dougie shouted from the stage as the crowd kept laughing.

"What a grouch," Chet muttered as he bit the last Popsicle chunk off the stick.

Dougie told his last joke, then left the stage. As another jester took his place, Iola began walking away too.

"Where you going?" Chet called after Iola.

"To look for my friends," Iola called back. "At least *they* won't embarrass me."

Joe looked beyond Chet's shoulder and smiled. "Speaking of friends," he said. "Here comes Phil."

Frank turned to see Phil Cohen walking over. Phil's green feathered cap reminded Frank of Robin Hood.

"Hi," Frank said. He nodded at a blue sheet of paper in Phil's hand. "What's that?"

"It's a list for the Squire's Scavenger Hunt,"

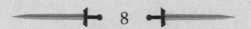

Phil said, his eyes flashing. "I have to find everything on it in order to win."

"Cool," Joe said.

"Hey, I know!" Phil said. "Why don't you guys join the scavenger hunt so we could be a team?"

"Not unless there's food on the list," Chet said.

"Frank and I can't either," Joe said. "We're entering the Junior Joust Competition."

"Joust?" Phil said, his eyes widening. "You mean you're going to knock each other off horses with those long spearlike things?"

"They're called lances," Frank said. "And you're talking about the real knights' joust that's later today."

"We're entering the *Junior* Joust," Joe explained. "We're lancing a ring hanging from a tree. And our horse is a fake horse pulled with a rope."

"The best part is the grand prize," Frank said.

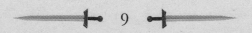

"The winner and a couple of friends get to watch the knights' joust with King Arthur himself!"

"Why don't you enter the Junior Joust, Phil?" Joe asked. "You like figuring things out. Maybe you can figure out how to lance the ring!"

"Thanks, but I'll pass," Phil said. "I want to find the first thing on this list. It's a Popsicle stick."

Chet handed Phil his Popsicle stick and said, "Consider it found!"

"Thanks, Chet!" Phil said happily. He dropped the wooden stick into his pocket, gave a wave, and hurried off.

"Huzzah!" a voice boomed.

Frank, Joe, and Chet turned to see a fair crier wearing a colorful banner over his tunic. On it were the words JUNIOR JOUST.

"Come ye all to the Junior Joust!" the crier shouted as he walked by. "Don't be late, or suffer the fate!"

"The Junior Joust," Frank said excitedly. "This is it, Joe!"

"Chet, are you in too?" Joe asked.

"Sure," Chet said. He nodded at the next jester on the stage. "These jokes are as old as King Arthur himself!"

The brothers and Chet followed signs to the joust track. Once there, they saw a fake horse tethered to a rope. The track ran under a row of trees. From one tree dangled a gold ring.

A bunch of kids had already lined up. Frank, Joe, and Chet grabbed places at the back of the line. The contest was about to start when—

"Hey!" Joe complained.

Three taller boys pushed past Frank, Joe, and Chet. When the Hardys and Chet saw who the taller boys were, they frowned.

The biggest guy was Adam Ackerman, the bully of Bayport Elementary School. Standing

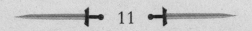

with Adam were his friends Tony Riccio and Seth Darnell. All three wore belted medieval tunics and sneaky smiles.

"What do you want, Adam?" Frank asked.

"I want you to step aside," Adam declared. He narrowed his eyes and added, "Or prepare to face our wrath!"

Ring Zinger

Frank, Joe, and Chet traded frowns. This wasn't the first time Adam had tried to spoil their fun.

"What are you doing here, Ackerman?" Joe said. He pointed to the stuffed fake horse. "This game already has a horse's butt."

"Very funny!" Adam said. He stood over Joe, glaring down into his eyes.

CLANG, CLANG, CLANG!

The boys glanced sideways to see that a figure

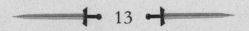

dressed in full armor was lumbering straight toward them. His face was covered with a visor, and his helmet was topped with a red plume.

"It's one of the knights!" Chet said.

The knight stopped before Adam and put his steely hands on his hips. Adam stared at the knight, then stepped away from Joe.

"Who needs this dumb game anyway?" Adam grumbled. He turned to his friends and said, "Let's get out of here."

"Good idea," Frank said.

Adam, Seth, and Tony stomped away. But before Joe could thank the knight, he was gone!

"Who was that guy, anyway?" Chet asked.

"Must be our lucky knight," Joe said with a smile. "I think I shall call him Sir Thanksalot!"

The line moved quickly, but not quickly enough. Frank, Joe, and Chet couldn't wait to get their hands on the lance!

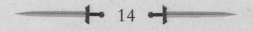

But not every kid was able to compete. A pair of twins stood arguing with the squire in charge of the game.

"Why can't we play?" one boy cried.

"You're too young for this contest," the squire said. "And too small."

"Then give us a bigger stick!" the other boy demanded.

"Rules are rules," the squire told the twins.

Frank, Joe, and Chet recognized the twins. They were Matty and Scotty Zamora. The Zamora family owned the best pizza parlor in Bayport.

"I heard the Zamoras have a pizza stand here at the fair," Frank said. "They even have some kind of contest."

"What kind of contest?" Joe asked.

"The kid who pulls a sword out of a giant hunk of cheese wins free pizza for a month," Frank explained.

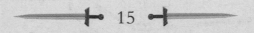

"Free pizza for a month?" Chet exclaimed. He nodded at the joust. "And they call *this* the grand prize?"

The boys inched their way to the front of the line. It was Frank's turn first. He climbed up onto the fake horse and grabbed the lance.

"Charge!" Frank shouted when he was ready.

A man dressed as a medieval stableman stood at the other side of the track. He pulled the rope attached to the horse. The fake horse jerked forward, then took off.

"Go, Frank!" Joe cheered as the horse carried Frank down the track. Frank aimed his lance at the ring dangling from the tree, but he missed.

"Rats!" Frank complained.

Next was Joe's turn.

"Watch this!" Joe said as he climbed up onto the horse. But when he aimed his lance at the ring, he missed too.

"It's harder than it looks, Chet," Joe said as he jumped down from the horse.

"No problem. I've got this!" Chet said as he climbed up. He grabbed the lance and shouted, "Chaaaaaaarge!"

Frank and Joe watched Chet ride the fake horse down the track. As he neared the ring, he coolly lifted the lance and—

"He nailed it!" Joe shouted.

"Chet was the first to lance the gold ring!" Frank cheered. "He won the grand prize!"

The crowd cheered as Chet hopped off the horse. The gold ring circled the lance as he waved it high in the air.

"How did you do it, Chet?" Frank asked.

"Easy," Chet said with a smile. "I pictured the ring as a chocolate glazed donut with sprinkles!"

But not everyone was happy for Chet.

"It's not fair!" Scotty complained. "We didn't even get a chance!"

"We would have won if it wasn't for him!" Matty said, pointing at Chet.

"Come back after you've grown a few inches," Joe suggested.

The twins scowled at Joe, then walked away.

"Hold on to that ring," the squire told Chet, "and present it to King Arthur at the knights' joust later."

"You mean the big joust with real knights?" Chet exclaimed. "Awesome."

Frank, Joe, and Chet left the jousting track.

"What should we do next?" Joe asked.

"Let's try the sword-in-the-cheese contest

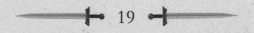

with the free pizza prize," Chet suggested. "I'm feeling lucky!"

"You mean hungry!" Frank teased.

The boys followed signs to the Royal Food Court. On the way they passed a life-size game of chess, a juggler juggling fiery torches, and a parade of giant puppets. Once at the food court Chet followed the cheesy pizza smells to the Zamoras' stand.

Behind the stand stood nine-year-old Daisy Zamora, helping her parents. Daisy was a fourth grader at Bayport Elementary School just like Frank and Chet.

"Sorry your brothers didn't get the ring," Joe said to Daisy.

Daisy rolled her eyes as she busily handed out pizza slices.

"They said they were going to some pie eating contest, so they are already over it," Daisy said. "As if they aren't messy enough!"

"Pies sound good to me too," Chet said. "But where can we find that sword-in-the-cheese contest?"

"Right in the back!" Mr. Zamora called over his shoulder as he flipped a huge slab of dough in the air.

"Good luck," Daisy said with a smile. "You're going to need it!"

Frank, Joe, and Chet walked around to the back. They saw a huge hunk of cheese held to the ground by spikes and ropes. Sticking out of the cheese, handle-side up, was a sword!

"I'll go first," Chet said. He handed Frank the gold ring. "Hold my grand prize while I try."

Frank and Joe stood under a shady tree while Chet stepped up to the cheese. He shook out his shoulders and spit on both hands. Then, feet spread apart, Chet grabbed the handle tight.

"Go, Chet!" Joe cheered.

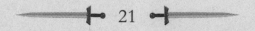

Chet grunted as he pulled and pulled. The cheese shook, but the sword refused to budge!

"Here," Frank said, giving the ring to Joe. "Hold this while I help Chet."

"Go for it," Joe said.

Holding the prize gold ring, Joe sat down under the tree. He watched as his brother and friend struggled with the sword.

Joe wanted to help too, but what would he do with the ring? Glancing up, Joe saw a tree branch over his head.

"Perfect!" Joe said. He stood up on his toes to reach the branch. After slipping the ring onto it, he ran over to the cheese.

"Let me try!" Joe said.

Now three pairs of hands clutched the handle. Frank, Joe, and Chet grunted as they pulled at the stubborn sword.

"Hey," a voice called.

Frank, Joe, and
Chet looked up. It was
their friend Phil
Cohen again.

"Want some
help?" Phil asked.

"Thanks . . . but . . . we . . .
got . . . this!" Chet grunted.

"Okay," Phil said
before walking
away. "Good luck!"

"We've . . .
heard . . . that . . .
before!" Joe
grunted.

The Hardys and Chet tried some more. Joe stuck his foot onto the cheese for support. No matter how hard they pulled, they couldn't get the sword out of the cheese!

After another minute the boys gave up.

"I thought I was lucky!" Chet groaned.

"Cheer up, Chet," Joe said. "You can't be the big cheese every time."

"Cute," Chet laughed. "Okay, where's my prize ring?"

Joe turned to point at the tree.

"It's right over th—" Joe stopped midsentence. His jaw dropped. The grand prize gold ring that he'd hung on the tree was *gone*!

Grand Prize Goner

Um . . . it was over here," Joe said, rushing to the empty tree branch. "Maybe it fell off!"

Joe's heart pounded as he looked down. There was no gold ring on the ground anywhere!

"What are you talking about, Joe?" Chet said. "I gave the gold ring to Frank, not you."

"I gave it to Joe, Chet," Frank said. "So I could help you with the sword."

"And I hung it on this tree branch so I could help too," Joe said. "But it's not here."

"Then where'd it go?" Chet cried. "How could you have put it somewhere for anyone to steal, Joe?"

"You think somebody stole it?" Joe said, wide-eyed.

"Who wouldn't want the grand prize?" Chet wailed. "Thanks a lot, Joe. Now we'll never see the joust with King Arthur." Chet shook his head in disbelief. Then, without saying good-bye, he walked away.

"I should have held on to that ring," Frank said.

"And I shouldn't have hung it on that branch," Joe muttered. "Now I lost the grand prize *and* our friend!"

"Who said the ring is lost?" Frank said, turning to Joe. "I think it was stolen too, just like Chet said."

"What do we do about it?" Joe asked.

"We find the ring before the knights' joust, that's what," Frank said. "But first we find the *thief.*"

Joe cracked a small smile. He knew what that meant. The Hardy brothers were on the case!

"Let's go back to our tree house, Frank," Joe said. "We can write our suspects and clues on our Secret Files board. We can ask Dad for help too."

Frank gave it a thought. Fenton Hardy ran a busy detective agency but was never too busy to help them with their cases. Their mom Laura was a real estate agent. She knew every block in Bayport, which also came in handy.

"There's no time," Frank said, shaking his head. "And we don't know where Aunt Gertrude is to drive us back."

"No problem," Joe decided. He looked around for something to write with. He grabbed a twig and carved the word "suspects" into a patch of dirt.

"The person who stole Chet's ring could have been anybody here at the fair," Frank decided. "Who wouldn't want the grand prize?"

Joe looked around. The sword-in-the-cheese and the tree were in an out-of-the-way place.

"Somebody could have followed us here," Joe suggested. "But who?"

"What about Matty and Scotty?" Frank asked. "They were acting like the prize should have been theirs."

"But Daisy said the twins went to some pie eating contest," Joe said.

"That's where they *said* they were going," Frank pointed out. "They could have been secretly hanging out back here watching us."

"Those twins were always trouble times two!" Joe said as he scratched the twins names into the dirt.

"Speaking of trouble," Frank said. "What about Adam Ackerman? He and his friends looked mad when Sir Thanksalot scared them away."

"Mad enough to get even," Joe said, and sighed. "That's Adam!"

Joe added Adam's name to the list. "We have

our first suspects," Joe said. "Now where do we look for clues?"

"How about at the scene of the crime?" Frank suggested.

The brothers went back to the tree. They looked down around the tree's thick roots.

"This tree is surrounded by grass," Frank pointed out. "Footprints are going to be hard to find."

"Who needs footprints?" Joe said with a smile. "I think I found something better!"

Joe kneeled down. He pointed to something shining in the grass. Brushing aside the grass, he picked up a small round silver bell.

"It could have been there before we got here," Frank said.

"It wasn't!" Joe insisted.

"How do you know?" Frank asked.

"Because I was sitting down in that same spot," Joe explained. "If I'd sat on a bell, I would have known it!"

"Okay, but what does a bell have to do with Adam?" Frank asked. "Or Matty and Scotty?"

"Maybe the bell belonged to some other suspect," Joe figured. "But who?"

As Joe dropped the bell into his pocket, a rustling noise interrupted his thoughts. Frank heard it too. The brothers turned to see a knight peeking out from behind a tree in the distance.

"Hello?" Joe called.

The knight ducked behind the tree. All that stuck out was the red plume on his helmet.

"Didn't Sir Thanksalot have a red feather on his helmet?" Frank asked in a low voice.

Joe nodded just as Sir Thanksalot slipped out from behind the tree and hurried away. It wasn't long before the mysterious knight disappeared into the crowd.

"That was weird," Frank said. "It's as if Sir Thanksalot were watching us."

"Yeah," Joe said. "But why?"

4

Bell Boy

The brothers decided not to look for Sir Thanksalot. They had a missing prize ring to find. But first Joe had a giant turkey leg to buy for lunch!

"Let's see Sir Thanksalot eat this through his helmet!" Joe said, waving the gargantuan drumstick.

"I still can't figure out what he wants," Frank said. "And why he followed us like that."

Joe nodded in agreement.

"I know Sir Thanksalot saved us from Adam," Joe said, "but he's turning into a real knight-mare. Get it?"

"Give it up, Joe," Frank said with a groan. "The jester contest is over."

Jester contest?

"Frank, the bell!" Joe said.

"What about it?" Frank asked.

"Dougie had bells on his cap and shoes," Joe remembered. "And Chet ruined Dougie's jokes by calling out the answers."

"Dougie also said Chet would be sorry," Frank replied. "Maybe he got even by stealing Chet's prize."

"And dropped one of his bells in the act!" Joe said. "What do you think, Frank?"

"I think we'd better find Dougie Skulnick," Frank said.

The brothers raced to the stage. The Jester Joke Slam contest was over. Only one kid stood juggling beanbags near the stage.

"Hi," Frank said. "Do you remember a guy named Dougie from the joke contest?"

The boy kept on juggling, his eyes pinned on the whirling beanbags. "Sure, I remember Dougie," he said.

"Where'd he go?" Joe asked.

"Last time I saw Dougie, he was going into Falcon Forest," the boy said, still juggling. "He said something about a ring—"

"A ring?" Joe gasped.

"Which way is Falcon Forest?" Frank asked.

"How can I point when I'm juggling?" the boy complained. "Follow the signs and you'll find it."

"Uh, thanks, I guess," Frank said as he and

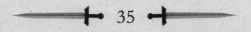

Joe left the kid, still juggling beanbags.

"So Dougie *did* say something about a ring," Joe said after chomping into his turkey leg. "Frank, this is huge!"

"So is that drumstick!" Frank joked. "Now let's look for Falcon Forest."

All through the park were wooden signs shaped like arrows. A green one pointed toward Falcon Forest. Frank and Joe found the forest a few feet away. Another arrow pointed to the opening, a pebbly path leading into the forest.

The brothers were nearing the opening when Joe stopped. He put his hand to his ear.

"Frank, did you hear that?" Joe asked. "It sounds like bells inside the forest."

Frank listened closely. He heard it too.

"Dougie was wearing bells," Frank said. "That could be him in there!"

Joe waved his drumstick at the opening and said, "Come on, Frank. Let's go!"

"Wait!" Frank said. He pointed to another sign that read NO BELLY TIMBER. "What do you think it means?"

Joe read the sign and shrugged.

"We've got some turkey, but we've got no timber in our bellies," Joe said. He used the turkey leg to point to the opening. "Now let's get our man!"

The brothers followed a pebbly path into the thick green forest. They saw other guests exploring the forest, but no Dougie.

"I kuhh I hane, ank," Joe mumbled, taking another bite of his turkey leg. "I heard em ow and cur."

"I can't understand you with your mouth full!" Frank complained.

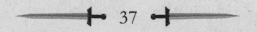

Frank was about to call Dougie's name when another sound filled the air—a loud fluttering sound.

"What's that?" Frank whispered.

Joe and Frank paused.

Joe waved his hand. "Probably nothing, just some wind or—"

Suddenly Joe's hand froze around the drum-

stick. The fluttering sound grew louder and louder. It seemed like it was getting closer and closer to the boys. Until—

Screech, screeeeeeeech!

Frank and Joe stared straight ahead, openmouthed. Swooping toward them was a giant bird with an enormous wingspan and needle-sharp talons!

"Aaaah!" Joe shouted. "Bird attack!"

5

Brave the Cave

A man dressed in a leather tunic burst out from between some trees. He grasped a thin rope attached to the bird's foot.

"Drop the drumstick, kid!" he shouted. "Drop the drumstick!"

Joe dropped his giant turkey leg onto the ground. The bird swooped down onto it. A small bell tied to the bird's foot jingled as he pecked.

"That's all he wanted," the man said, sighing.

Frank and Joe looked up at the man, tethered to the bird.

"Who are you?" Frank asked.

"I'm John, the falconer," the man replied. "I handle most of the falcons in this forest."

"Oh yeah?" Joe said. He nodded down at the bird, still eating heartily. "How come you couldn't handle this guy?"

"How come you didn't read the sign?" John asked. He pointed down at the drumstick. "No belly timber allowed!"

"'Belly timber' means 'food'?" Frank asked.

"It did in the Middle Ages," John said.

"We don't talk Middle Age!" Joe exclaimed. He looked down at the falcon. "And why does that bird have a bell on his foot?"

"All of the falcons here have bells on their legs," John explained. "It's how we track them in case they fly away. Falconers have been doing it that way since the time of King Arthur."

"We thought the bell belonged to a jester we were looking for," Frank explained.

"You didn't happen to see a kid jester here in the forest," Joe asked John, "did you?"

"Come to think of it," John said, rubbing his chin thoughtfully, "there was a kid dressed like a jester here about an hour ago."

"Seriously?" Joe said excitedly.

"What was he doing?" Frank asked.

"He was just walking through the forest," John said. "He stopped to pet one of the falcons."

"Did the jester say anything?" Joe asked.

"Just something about taking a shortcut," John explained. "But he never said where he was going."

Frank wanted to ask John if the jester was carrying a gold ring, until the falcon flapped its wings and took off.

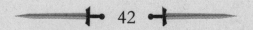

"Gotta fly!" John joked. Then, holding his end of the rope, he hurried after the falcon through the forest.

"Thanks for your help!" Joe called after him. He looked down at the eaten drumstick and said, "Oh, and keep the belly timber."

The brothers hurried down the forest path. They could see a light up ahead, and they knew they'd found the way out of the forest.

When they finally made their way to the end of the path, Frank and Joe looked around.

"There he is!" Joe shouted. He pointed to Dougie standing in the near distance. Dougie was wearing his jester costume and holding something gold in his hand.

"Chet's ring!" Frank exclaimed.

The brothers raced toward Dougie.

"What's up?" Dougie asked, twirling the big ring on his index finger.

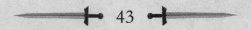

"We want that ring you're spinning," Joe replied. He held out his hand and said, "So why don't you put it right there?"

"No way," Dougie complained. "Get your own ring!"

"There's only one grand prize, and you know it, Dougie," Frank said. "It was won by Chet Morton."

"Did you steal Chet's prize ring or not?" Joe asked.

"I didn't steal anything," Dougie insisted.

"Then what's that?" Joe said, pointing to the ring on Dougie's finger.

"Huzzah!" a voice boomed.

The boys turned to see another crier. He cupped his hands around his mouth as he shouted, "Prepare ye all for the Royal Ring Toss. The Royal Ring Toss shall begin!"

"Yes!" Dougie cheered under his breath. "I'm going to ace the ring toss contest this year."

"Ring toss?" Frank said.

"Contest?" Joe asked.

Dougie nodded as he handed Joe the ring.

"I picked this one from the ring toss bucket," Dougie said. "It looks lucky, don't you think?"

Frank and Joe studied the ring. It was wrapped with a dark red ribbon. Chet's ring had no ribbon around it.

"It looks smaller than Chet's ring too," Joe said.

"That's because it's not Chet's ring," Dougie said. "Why would I want to steal Chet's prize anyway?"

"Because he ruined your act?" Frank suggested.

"Ruined?" Dougie said. He shook his head. "Chet helped me win the Jester Joke Slam!"

"You mean you won?" Frank asked.

"Even with Chet yelling out the answers to your jokes?" Joe said.

"Chet is why I won," Dougie explained. "Everyone thought he was part of the act."

"So you weren't mad at him?" Joe asked.

"Mad at Chet?" Dougie said. The bells on his cap jangled as he shook his head. "I should thank him."

Frank and Joe watched Dougie race to the ring toss field. Why would Dougie want revenge on Chet if he had helped him win?

"I checked out the bells on Dougie's cap and shoes," Frank added. "They were blue, not silver like the one you found."

"So Dougie didn't steal Chet's prize ring," Joe said, and sighed. "I guess the joke was on us!"

Frank and Joe wanted to watch the ring toss contest, but they had work to do.

"Time is running out," Frank said. "We have to find the ring thief before the knights' joust."

"Speaking of knights," Joe said, looking past Frank. "There's our worst knight-mare."

Frank turned around and frowned. It was Sir Thanksalot, following them again!

Joe spotted a cave opening cut into a rocky mountainside. According to a sign, it was the Dragon Cave.

"Come on, Frank," Joe said. "Let's lose that tin man!"

Frank and Joe slipped into the cave. It was dark, but they could make out some chalk drawings on the stone walls. The pictures were all of fire-breathing dragons.

"Let's go deeper into the cave, Joe," Frank suggested. "Just in case Thanksalot decides to come in here too!"

The brothers walked down a cool, dark tunnel.

"Do you think there's a dragon in here?" Joe asked. "Why else would they call it the Dragon Cave?"

"Give me a break," Frank said with a grin. "There's no such thing as—"

Frank stopped midsentence as laughter echoed through the tunnel. The brothers froze. They listened as the laughing voices began to speak. . . .

"Morton didn't have a clue we took it!" a boy said, and snickered.

"Yeah." Another boy chuckled. "We just grabbed it and ran!"

Frank and Joe traded stares.

"I know those voices," Frank whispered.

"Me too," Joe whispered back. "It's Adam and his friends—and they stole something from Chet!"

The Pits!

Frank and Joe heard footsteps. They flattened themselves against a wall as three shadowy figures rushed past them through the tunnel.

The brothers raced to the mouth of the cave. They looked outside. Adam and his friends were walking away.

When Adam stopped to buy a snow cone, Joe spotted something that made his jaw drop. A medieval-style pouch was hanging from Adam's shoulder. Inside the pouch was the outline of a ring!

"Adam's got Chet's ring!" Joe exclaimed. "And it's in that bag!"

Frank and Joe shouted Adam's name as they charged toward the snow cone stand.

"We know what you stole, Ackerman!" Frank said.

"Give it back!" Joe demanded.

Adam, Seth, and Tony spun around, snow cones in their hands.

"What are you talking about?" Adam demanded.

"That thing you said you stole from Morton," Joe repeated. "We want it!"

Cracking a small smile, Adam said, "You want it? Come get it!"

Adam handed his snow cone to Tony, then took off.

"Two snow cones!" Tony exclaimed. "Am I lucky or what?"

Frank and Joe didn't feel lucky. Adam was getting away with Chet's ring!

"We've got to get him!" Frank declared.

Frank and Joe ran as fast as they could. They chased Adam through a giant puppet parade, an acrobat show, and the archery court. They were about to dart across the human chessboard when the brothers screeched to a stop.

"Frank," Joe said, trying to catch his breath, "do you see what I see?"

Frank nodded as he panted too. Adam was entering the Medieval Maze!

Joe stared at the maze. Jumping over the muck pit wouldn't be easy, but how else were they going to try and catch Adam?

"We're going in too, Frank!" Joe insisted.

"Great," Frank groaned as they ran toward the gate. "Muck pit, here we come!"

Joe was inside the maze first. He could see Adam making his way across the rope bridge. First Joe had to crawl through the slinky Serpent Tunnel. He

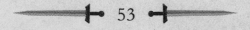

scrambled through the tunnel, as fast as lightning. Now he was just a few feet behind Adam.

The chase was on. Adam climbed over a wall, swung on a rope, and crawled under a fence made of painted tires. Joe did the same. But just as Joe was about to walk after Adam across a balance beam, another kid ran in front of him!

"Aw, come on!" Joe complained.

By the time Joe jumped off the beam, Adam was already at the final stop. Joe gulped. It was

the muck pit. Adam stood a few inches from the edge of the pit. He looked over his shoulder and shouted, "Game over, Hardy!"

Holding the bag, Adam took a few steps back. He then made a running jump and—*SPLAT!*

Joe couldn't believe his eyes. Adam Ackerman had fallen right into the mud!

"Arrrgh!" Adam cried.

The bag flew out of Adam's hand. It landed with a *CLUNK* on the other side of the muck pit. Joe stared across the pit at the bag. Adam was trying to stand up but kept slipping back down.

Frank caught up with Joe and shook his head. "Forget it," he said glumly. "I don't think you are going to catch up. Ask them to let you skip this part!"

"Skip it? No way!" Joe exclaimed. "I can do this!"

Joe ran back a few feet. He gritted his teeth, scrunched his fists, and ran for it. With a flying leap Joe made it across the muck pit to the other side!

"Go, Joe!" Frank shouted.

Joe picked up the bag. He waved it in the air and yelled, "Game still on, Ackerman!"

Adam slipped and slid in the muck pit as he tried to stand up.

"Coming through!" Frank shouted as he leaped over Adam and the muck pit too.

Frank and Joe traded a high five.

"We jumped the muck pit!" Joe cheered. He waved Adam's bag in the air. "And here's our prize!"

"Well?" Frank said with a smile. "Open it and take out the ring!"

Joe was about to pull the string on the bag when another voice growled, "Why don't you let me do it, Hardy-Har-Har?"

Joe gasped as the bag was yanked out of his hand. He turned and muttered, "Great."

Holding the bag was Adam. He was dripping from head to toe with mud—and anger!

A Blue Clue

Like I said earlier," Joe said as he looked Adam up and down, "what this fair needs is a mud monster."

Adam opened the bag and pulled out the ring. He waved it and said, "Is this what you're looking for?"

The brothers stared at the gold ring in Adam's hand. It didn't look like Chet's ring at all!

"That ring has colored stones on it," Joe murmured. "Chet's didn't."

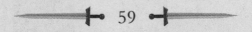

"Yeah, but that ring looks familiar," Frank murmured back. "Where did we see it before?"

"What are you whispering about?" Adam said with a frown. He held the ring in the air, until another hand reached out and—

"Gotcha!" a girl's voice said.

Frank and Joe smiled. The girl was Chet's sister Iola. Standing next to Iola was a tall man wearing a star-shaped badge on his medieval costume.

"This is my crown, Sheriff," Iola said, placing the gold ring onto her head.

"So that's where we saw that 'ring' before," Joe said. "It wasn't a ring—it was Iola's crown."

"The Morton that Adam was talking about was Iola," Frank said. "Not Chet."

The sheriff of the fair pointed to Adam and said, "Is this the boy who took your crown, Iola?"

"That's one of them," Iola said. "I knew it was Adam and his friends who snatched the crown right off my head."

"Whatever," Adam mumbled.

"Why don't we find your friends, Adam?" the sheriff said. "Then we can talk about proper behavior at the King Arthur Fair."

The brothers watched as Adam trudged off with the sheriff.

"Thanks for trying to get my crown back,"

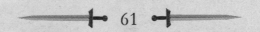

Iola said as she straightened her crown. "I saw you chasing Adam through the Medieval Maze."

"No problem, Your Majesty," Joe joked.

Iola smiled as she walked away. Frank and Joe began walking away too.

"I guess Adam's clean," Frank said.

"Are you kidding?" Joe joked. "He was dripping with mud!"

"Adam was innocent, Joe," Frank said. "And we still don't have Chet's prize ring."

"But we *did* get to run through the Medieval Maze *and* jump the muck pit!" Joe said with a grin.

All that running had made the brothers hungry, so they headed straight to the Zamoras' pizza stand. There they saw Chet walking away with a slice on a paper plate. Chet glanced at the Hardys, then kept walking.

"He's still mad at us," Joe said.

"He'll be mad at us until we find his ring," Frank said. He looked at his watch. "And we'd better find it soon, because the joust is in less than two hours."

Frank and Joe still had two suspects: Matty and Scotty, the Zamora twins. They didn't see the twins around the pizza stand, just Daisy helping her parents again.

"Hi, Daisy," Frank said. "Do you know where your little brothers are?"

"Do I have to?" Daisy joked.

Daisy's mom turned around from cutting a fresh pie into slices. "I know where the boys are," she said. "I just dropped them off at the medieval playground."

"Thanks, Mrs. Zamora!" Frank said.

"So, do you guys want slices?" Daisy asked.

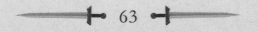

"We just took a pepperoni pie out of the oven."

"Yes!" Joe said.

"No, thanks," Frank said. "We'll be back later."

"Aw, Frank," Joe said as they headed toward the playground. "Why couldn't we get pizza first?"

"Like I said, time is running out," Frank said. "We have to talk to the twins now."

The brothers reached the medieval playground. Kids were playing on a dragon slide and a small unicorn merry-go-round.

"Where's Matty and Scott?" Joe asked.

"There!" Frank said.

Joe turned to see where Frank was pointing. The two heads of Matty and Scotty were bobbing up and down inside a colorful bouncy castle.

"We're going in," Frank said.

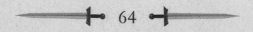

"Oh, no, we're not!" Joe said. "That thing is for little kids!"

"Stop acting like a little kid, and let's go!" Frank insisted.

"Okay," Joe said. "But I refuse to bounce!"

The castle itself was bouncing with kids when the brothers walked inside. They went straight to Matty and Scotty. The twins were throwing foam balls at each other as they were bouncing.

"Can we ask you something?" Joe said.

"Ask us what?" Scotty said.

"Where did you go after the Junior Joust?" Frank asked. "The one where our friend Chet won the big prize."

"The prize that should have been ours!" Scotty said.

"How can we forget where we went?" Matty

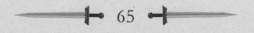

said. "Those blueberry pies were yummy-yummy-for-the-tummy!"

Joe remembered what Daisy had told them before. "You mean you were at the pie eating contest?" he asked the twins.

"Where else?" Matty said.

The twins stopped bouncing to do somersaults. When they rolled out of earshot, the Hardy brothers discussed the situation.

"Daisy told us the twins were at a pie eating contest," Joe said. "Right around the time I hung the ring on the tree."

"How do we know Matty and Scotty really went to the pie eating contest?" Frank said.

Joe gave it a thought, then smiled. "Did they say they had blueberry pie?" he asked.

"Yeah, so?" Frank replied.

"So, watch this," Joe said. He turned to the

twins and shouted, "Hey, Matty, Scotty!"

When the twins looked over, Joe stuck out his tongue and yelled, "Blaaaaaaah!"

Matty and Scotty traded surprised looks. They then narrowed their eyes, stuck out their own tongues, and yelled, "Blaaaaah!"

"Frank, did you see that?" Joe hissed after the twins began bouncing again.

"Yeah, their tongues were blue," Frank said. "Probably from eating all those blueberry pies."

"I just thought of something else," Joe said. "Those kids are shorter than me."

"So?" Frank asked.

"So they couldn't have reached that tree branch," Joe explained. "Even I had to stand on my toes."

The brothers left the twins, still bouncing. The Hardy boys squeezed through more kids until they were finally outside the castle.

"Matty and Scotty were the last of our suspects," Frank said. "What now?"

CLANG, CLANG, CLANG!

Frank and Joe spun around. The mysterious knight with the red plume was walking straight toward them—fast!

"Sir Thanksalot is coming after us!" Frank said.

"Sir Thanksalot?" Joe exclaimed. "You mean Sir *Creepalot*!"

Knight Fright

The brothers ran as they looked for a place to hide. They heard heavy footsteps behind them and the sound of clanging armor. Sir Thanksalot—or Creepalot—was chasing them!

"In there," Frank said. He pointed to a small stone tower with colorful banners hanging from its walls.

Hoping to lose Sir Creepalot, Frank and Joe darted through the door. A woman sat behind a table filled with booklets about the King Arthur Fair.

"Welcome to King Arthur's Information Center," the woman said with a grin. "Would you like a map of the fair?"

Joe spotted a spiral staircase leading up. He shook his head and said, "No, thanks. I think we know where we're going!"

Frank and Joe raced up the winding staircase. At the top was a door that led to the rooftop.

"He'll never find us up here," Joe said when he and Frank were outside. They looked down over the stone wall that surrounded the roof.

"I don't see him," Frank said. But just when he and Joe thought they were safe—

CLANG, CLANG! CLANG!

Frank and Joe both gulped. Sir Creepalot was coming up the stairs. Before they could look for another way out, the door swung open.

Sir Creepalot stood in the doorway, before noisily stepping outside.

"Who are you?" Frank demanded.

"What do you want?" Joe asked in his bravest voice.

The knight reached up. He lifted his visor to uncover his face. Frank and Joe gasped. His face was *her* face.

"Aunt Gertrude?" Frank and Joe exclaimed.

"Hi, guys!" Aunt Gertrude said, grinning inside her helmet. "Surprised?"

Frank and Joe stared, openmouthed. All this time the mysterious knight had been their aunt?

"Why are you dressed up as a knight?" Frank asked. "And why were you following us all through the fair?"

"And why didn't you let us know it was you, Aunt Gertrude?" Joe asked.

Aunt Gertrude chuckled at all the questions.

"I wanted to keep an eye on you after I dropped you off here at the fair," Aunt Gertrude explained. "I didn't want you to know, so I rented a suit of armor as a disguise!"

"Wow," Frank said, shaking his head in

disbelief. "I never pictured you as a knight, Aunt Gertrude."

"Well, I always wanted to be a knight!" Aunt Gertrude laughed. "Do I look like a damsel in distress to you?"

The brothers shook their heads.

"Thanks for scaring Adam away at the Junior Joust, Aunt Gertrude," Joe said. "But did you have to chase us all the way up here?"

Aunt Gertrude nodded and said, "I wanted to tell you about a neat scavenger hunt here at the fair."

The brothers watched as Aunt Gertrude pulled a rolled-up piece of paper from her armored glove.

"Here's the list in case you want to play!" Aunt Gertrude said, handing it to Frank.

"Thanks, Aunt Gertrude," Frank said. "We already knew about the scavenger hunt from our friend Phil."

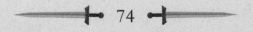

"Good!" Aunt Gertrude replied. "Now if you'll excuse me—I've got a few dragons to slay!"

Aunt Gertrude dropped her visor over her face. She turned noisily toward the door and left the castle roof.

"Bye, Aunt Gertrude!" Joe called. He turned to Frank, who was studying the list.

"This does look pretty cool," Frank admitted. "Phil has to find a pirate's eye patch, a cookie shaped like a dragon, a gold ring—" Frank stopped midsentence. He looked up at Joe, who was staring back at him.

"Frank?" Joe said slowly. "Did you just say *gold ring?*"

9

Spin or Lose

I t's right here on the list," Frank said. "Do you think somebody in the scavenger hunt took Chet's ring?"

"Phil's the only one we know in the scavenger hunt," Joe said. "He came around when we were trying to pull the sword out of the cheese!"

"That was when Chet's ring was hanging from the tree branch," Frank said. "He could have walked over to it while we were busy."

"It's not like he did anything wrong," Joe said.

"He couldn't have known it was Chet's ring."

Frank and Joe looked at the scavenger hunt list again.

"There's something else Phil had to find," Frank said. "A bell!"

Joe remembered the bell they'd found underneath the tree. "I think we found some pretty good things on this scavenger hunt too, Frank," he said.

"What?" Frank asked.

"Clues!" Joe said. "Now let's find Phil."

"Where?" Frank said. "Phil could be anywhere in the fair by now."

Joe knew Frank was right. But as he looked at the scavenger hunt list, he had a thought.

"The last thing Phil has to find is a ticket stub from the Spinning Barrel ride," Joe said.

Frank knew the Spinning Barrel at the fair. The barrel-shaped ride spun around so fast that everyone stuck to the sides.

"It's a long shot," Frank said. "But let's see if Phil is at the Spinning Barrel."

"Okay," Joe said. "But no way am I spinning like some sock in a washing machine!"

Frank looked at Joe as if to say, *We'll see.* Then they ran down the winding stairs and out of the tower.

The Spinning Barrel wasn't hard to find. It was with most of the other rides from the fair.

Frank and Joe saw a line of kids filing into the giant barrel. One of those kids was Phil. The brothers called Phil's name. When he didn't hear, Frank said, "We're going in there too."

"But I'll lose my lunch!" Joe complained.

"And if we don't go on the ride, we'll lose Phil!" Frank said. "Will you come on, Joe?"

"Great," Joe groaned under his breath as he followed Frank to the ticket booth.

After quickly buying tickets, they raced to the gate. When the ticket taker saw Joe, she raised an eyebrow and said, "Are you tall enough for this ride?"

Joe stood on his toes and said, "I am now!"

The brothers hurried into the barrel in the nick of time. Joe gulped as the heavy wooden door slammed shut behind them. There was no turning back!

"There's Phil!" Frank said.

Joe looked to see where Frank was pointing. On the other side of the barrel stood Phil. When Phil saw Frank and Joe, he waved them over.

"I heard this ride is awesome!" Phil said as the brothers took spots next to him.

"Are you sure you don't mean *awful*?" Joe joked.

"It's a good thing we found you, Phil," Frank said. "Chet's gold ring—"

"Around and around we gooooooo!" a booming voice interrupted.

Joe grabbed two handles on the wall at his sides. He squeezed his eyes shut as the barrel began to spin faster and faster!

"Look, guys!" Phil said, letting go of the handles. "No hands!"

"Hey, Phil!" Frank shouted over the yells and cheers. "Where's the stuff you found for the scavenger hunt?"

Phil shouted back as they stood plastered

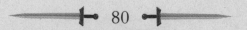

against the barrel: "I put them in a locker. Why?"

"The gold ring, too?" Joe shouted.

Phil's hand was stuck against the wall near the pocket of his jeans. He reached under his tunic and pulled out a gold ring!

"You mean this?" Phil shouted.

Frank and Joe stared at the ring. It looked exactly like Chet's grand prize!

"Where did you get it?" Joe shouted.

"It was hanging on some tree near the pizza stand," Phil shouted back. "Was I lucky or what?"

"What about a bell?" Frank shouted. "Did you lose a bell there too?"

Phil stared at Frank with surprise. "You found my bell?" he asked. "I knew I'd lost it but didn't know where."

"Phil, listen up!" Joe shouted as he got dizzier and dizzier. "That gold ring was Chet's. It was his grand prize for winning the Junior Joust."

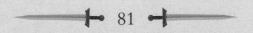

"No way!" Phil exclaimed. "I didn't know it was Chet's prize when I took it."

"We figured that," Frank said.

Phil looked down at the ring in his hand.

"Take this and give it to Chet," Phil said. "I'm sure I can find another ring somewhere around here."

Joe smiled as he stuck out his hand, as best he could. "Thanks, Phil," he said. "Put it right there!"

Phil held the ring out to Joe. But before Joe could grab it, the ring flew out of Phil's hand!

"Noooooo!" Frank shouted. He watched as the ring circled midair inside the spinning barrel.

"It's going to get sucked into a vortex!" Joe screamed, watching the ring. "A bottomless black hole!"

"Sorry, you guys!" Phil said.

The brothers looked across the barrel to the other side. Chet was jumping and reaching to try to grab the ring.

"Gotcha!" Chet yelled. He held up the gold ring and grinned from ear to ear!

10
Fit for a King

The barrel slowly came to a stop. As everyone filed out of the ride, Frank, Joe, and Phil ran over to Chet.

"Good catch!" Frank told Chet.

"It's all in the wrist," Chet joked. He held up the ring. "So is this my winning ring?"

"The one and only!" Joe declared.

"Cool!" Chet said. "How did you guys find it?"

"I had it, Chet," Phil explained. "I didn't

know it was your ring when I took it off the tree branch."

"Sorry, Chet," Joe said. "What was I thinking, leaving the ring on that tree branch?"

"Over it!" Chet said with a grin. "Hey, you got me my ring back."

Frank and Joe smiled. Not only had they gotten the ring back, they'd gotten their friend back. And that was the coolest!

"Now let's get off this thing," Joe said. "Before it starts spinning again!"

The boys stepped out of the Spinning Barrel ride. As Phil left to find a new ring, another crier walked past the boys.

"Huzzah!" the crier shouted. "The knights' joust is about to begin. Come ye all to the brave knights' joust!"

"What are we waiting for?" Chet asked, tossing

the ring back and forth. "The king awaits!"

Frank, Joe, and Chet raced to the royal box that overlooked the jousting field. King Arthur was already seated on his throne. Of course, the boys knew he wasn't the real King Arthur, but with his bejeweled crown and red velvet robe, he sure looked the part!

"Greetings, Your Majesty!" Joe said. He pointed to Chet holding the ring. "Our friend comes bearing bling."

The king's eyebrows flew up when he saw the ring. "Ah!" he said to Chet. "You must be the Junior Joust champ."

"I am, but these guys are champs too," Chet said. He pointed his thumb at Frank and Joe. "*Detective* champs!"

It wasn't long before Frank, Joe, and Chet were watching the knights' joust from the best seats at the fair. The boys sprang to their feet, cheering as one knight on horseback knocked the other knight's shield from his armored hand!

As the next knights took their places, Joe leaned

over to Frank and said, "There's something I want to do, Frank," Joe said. "Something important."

"Yeah? What?" Frank asked.

Joe smiled as he pointed down to the knights on horseback. "I want to find out if one of those knights," he said, "is really Aunt Gertrude!"

The boys laughed.

"There is something I need to do too," Frank said. "As soon as we get home, I want to write something on our tree house board. . . ."

SECRET FILES CASE #18: SOLVED!

Those jousting knights were pretty awesome, Joe.

True, but guess what?

We would have made great knights in those days too!

ARMOR

Us? Knights?

ARMOR

Sure! I'll prove it.

We're strong like knights.

. . . Almost as strong.

THIS WAY TO THE DRAGON

We can slay dragons like knights!

...Not *that* kind of dragon!

We're awesome at archery like knights.

Um... I meant archery video games.

I guess we *wouldn't* have made such great knights, Joe.

I just thought of something knights can do that we can do too!

Oh yeah? What?

-MEDIEVAL BANQUET- ALL YE CAN EAT!

Feast!

Huzzah!